Anna Obiols graduated from the University of Barcelona with a degree in History of Art. As well as being a writer, she now works in the children's section at a public library where she is responsible for organising activities to encourage children to read. Anna loves travelling. On her journeys she always tries to find exciting new people and places that she can bring together in her stories.

Subi is the pen name for Joan Subirana. He studied Applied Arts at university, and specialised in mural painting and graphic design. He now works as an illustrator for children's books and magazines, and has a daily comic strip in a newspaper in Catalonia. He has won many prizes in Spain for his illustrations, cartoons and paintings. Subi began drawing as a very young child, illustrating the stories he made up in his head. He believes that childhood is a precious time when everything is surprising and anything is possible, and he tries to keep that spirit alive in his paintings.

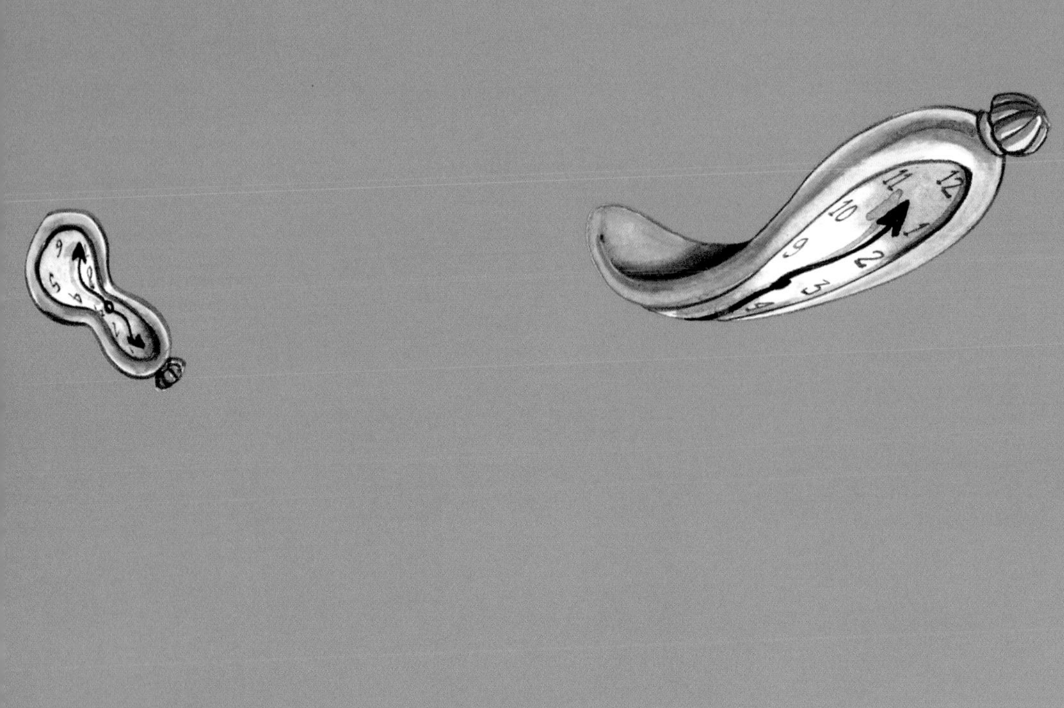
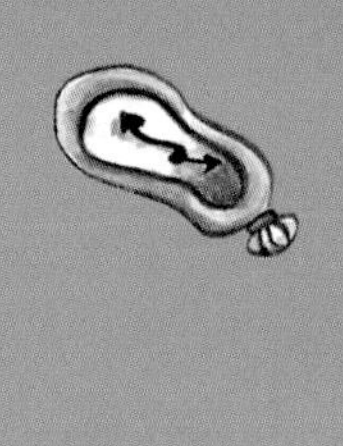
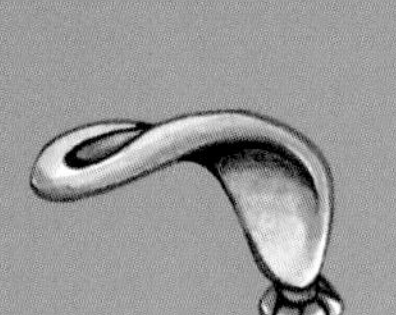
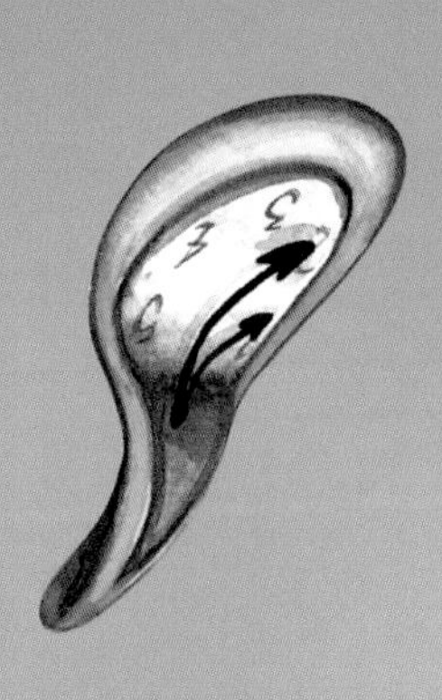
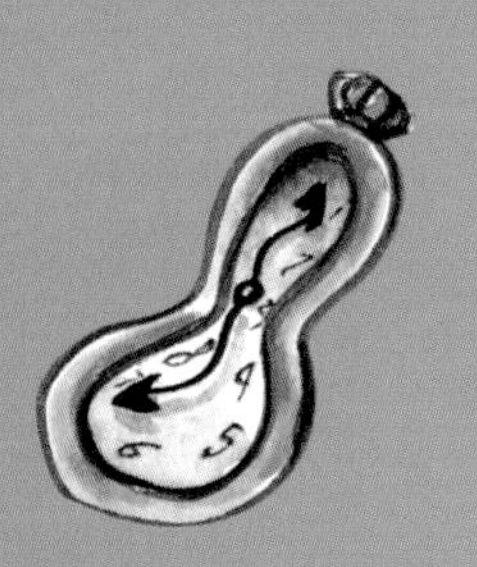
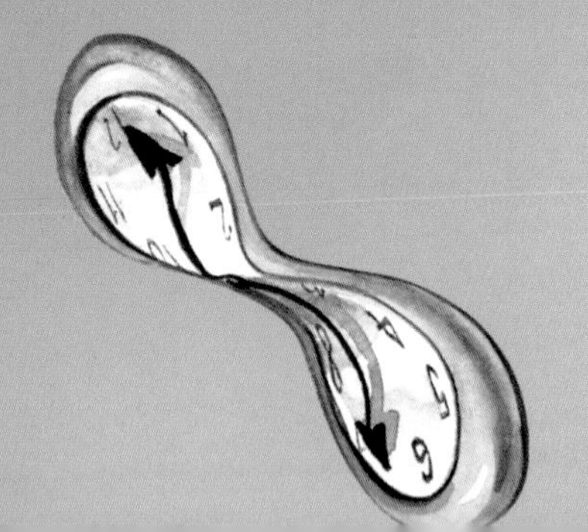

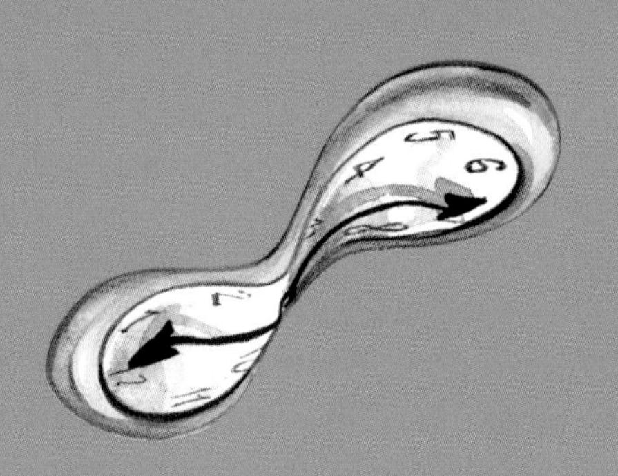
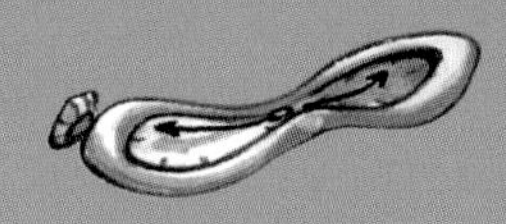

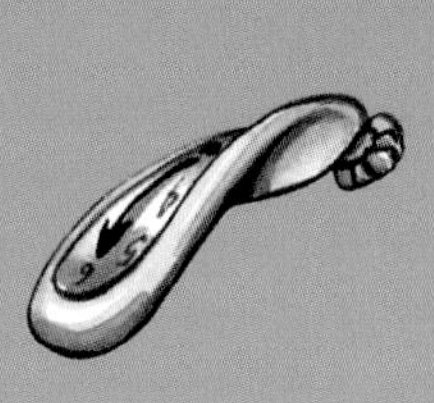
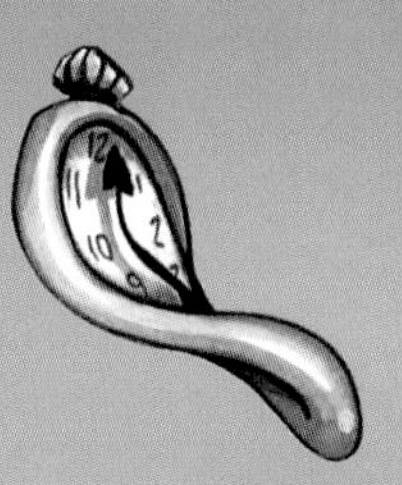
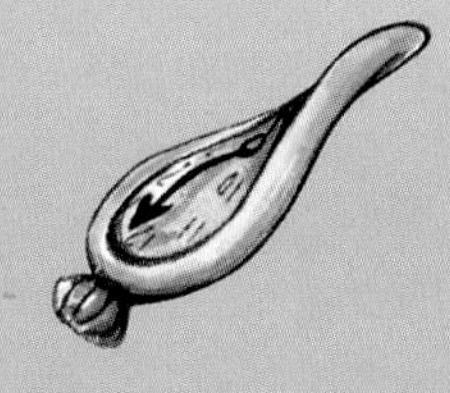
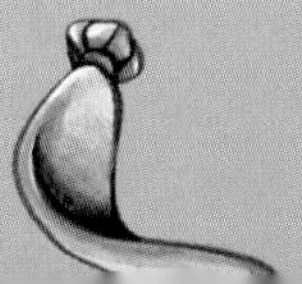

For little people with big dreams

A.O. – J.S.

On the centenary of the birth of Salvador Dalí,
we would like to pay tribute to this great painter by introducing his work to children.
This story is inspired by the marvellous fantasies that Dalí
left as his legacy to humanity.
Anna Obiols

In association with the Fundació Gala-Salvador Dalí

First published in Great Britain and the USA by in 2004 by
Frances Lincoln Children's Books, 4 Torriano Mews,
Torriano Avenue, London NW5 2RZ
www.franceslincoln.com

First published under the title El petit Dalí ... i el camí als somnis by Editorial Lumen,
Random House Mondadori, S.A., Spain

First paperback edition published in Great Britain and the USA in 2007

British Library Cataloguing in Publication Data available on request

ISBN 978-1-84507-777-8

Printed in Singapore by Tien Wah Press (Pte) Ltd. in September 2011

3 5 7 9 8 6 4

Dalí
and the Path of Dreams

Anna Obiols

Illustrated by Subi

English translation by Andrew Dunn

F

FRANCES LINCOLN
CHILDREN'S BOOKS

Once upon a time there was a little boy whose name was Salvador, though everyone called him Salvi. What Salvi liked most of all was to run barefoot along the beach with his hoop.

One afternoon, as he was playing in the waves, Salvi noticed something gleaming under the water. Looking closer, he saw it was a key that the sea had left there. Salvi popped it in his pocket.

Wondering what the key might be for,
Salvi hopped up on to his long-legged elephant
and let his imagination lead the way.

He soon came across a very strange cook who was tossing clocks as though they were pizzas. Each clock showed only one time and never changed. Suddenly, one of the clocks struck three, which was exactly the hour for magic.

"Hello, Cook!" said Salvi, "Do you know what this key is for?"

"Let's have a look," said the cook.

Salvi passed him the key.

"Ahaaa! This is a magic key! Leave your elephant here and get into this little boat – it knows where to take you."

Salvi was curious. He got into the boat, and immediately it began to float up into the air.

When he was nearer to the sky than the ground, Salvi noticed that some of the clouds made funny shapes like objects and animals, and he started to play at guessing what they looked like.

The boat floated up to a very tall tower that had seven enormous eggs on the roof. Salvi jumped out and ran up the steps that wound around the tower. He came to a very strange doorway.

Inside the tower
it was dark and mysterious.
Everywhere Salvi looked there were drawers
and doors. He wondered if he could open any of them,
but the key in his pocket didn't seem to fit any of the locks.

Salvi decided to try one last drawer.
This time, to his amazement, the key fitted.
Would he find a treasure chest? A secret map?
But inside there was just one black piano key.
Salvi popped it in his pocket, just as he had done
with the key from the sea.

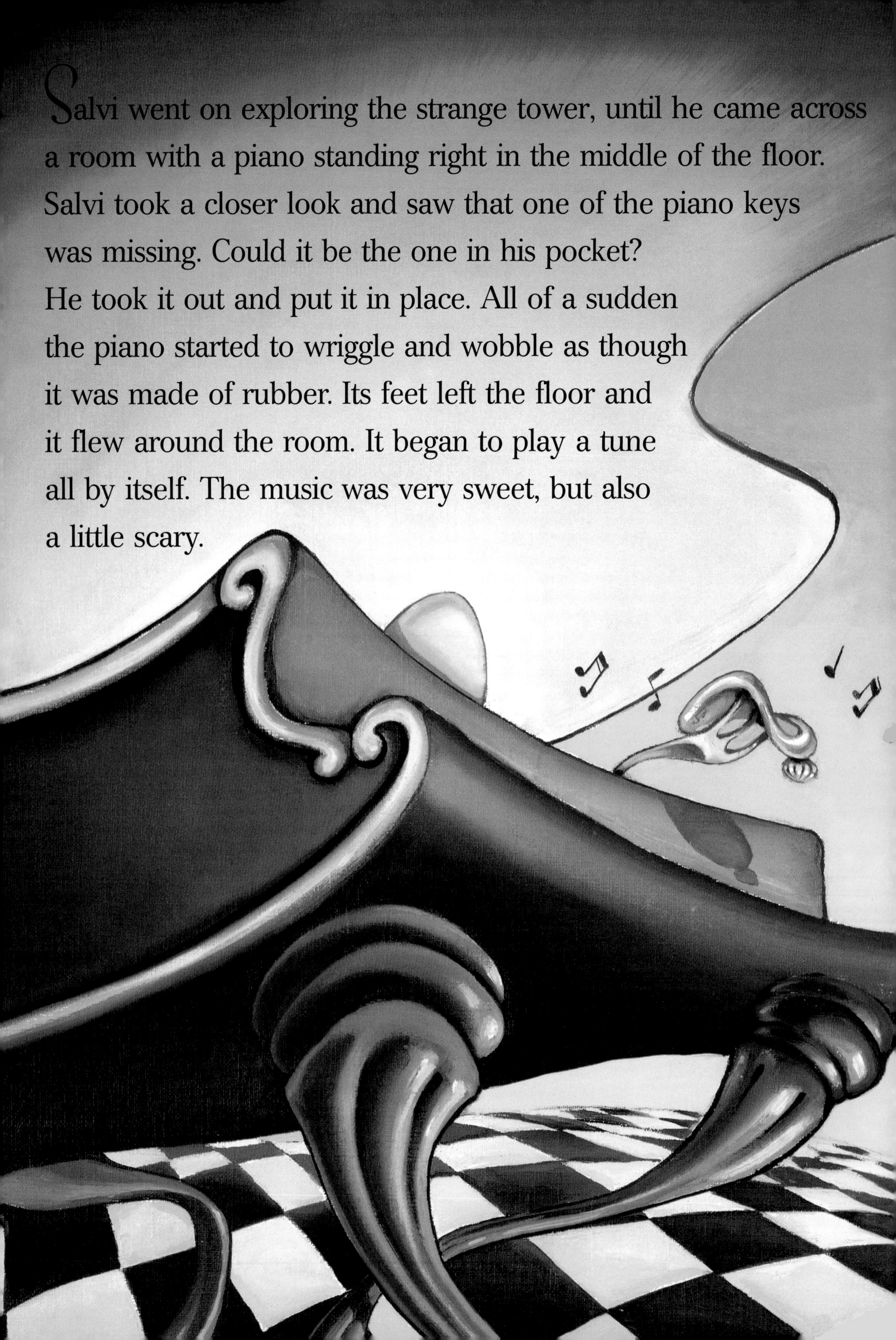

Salvi went on exploring the strange tower, until he came across a room with a piano standing right in the middle of the floor. Salvi took a closer look and saw that one of the piano keys was missing. Could it be the one in his pocket? He took it out and put it in place. All of a sudden the piano started to wriggle and wobble as though it was made of rubber. Its feet left the floor and it flew around the room. It began to play a tune all by itself. The music was very sweet, but also a little scary.

Then, in time to the music, a pawn, a swan, a snail-tamer, a flying banana and all sorts of strange people and objects appeared from the corners of the room.

The skipping lady, the fried-egg penguins,
the unicorn, the bread-head cyclist, the ants,
the stone man and the lady with butterfly wings
all set off along a very long path.

The path was so long it didn't seem to have any end as all, but at last it came to a point like the end of a long, black moustache. The point led to a very special drawer. Each and every one of these most peculiar people settled down to live in that drawer for a very long time.

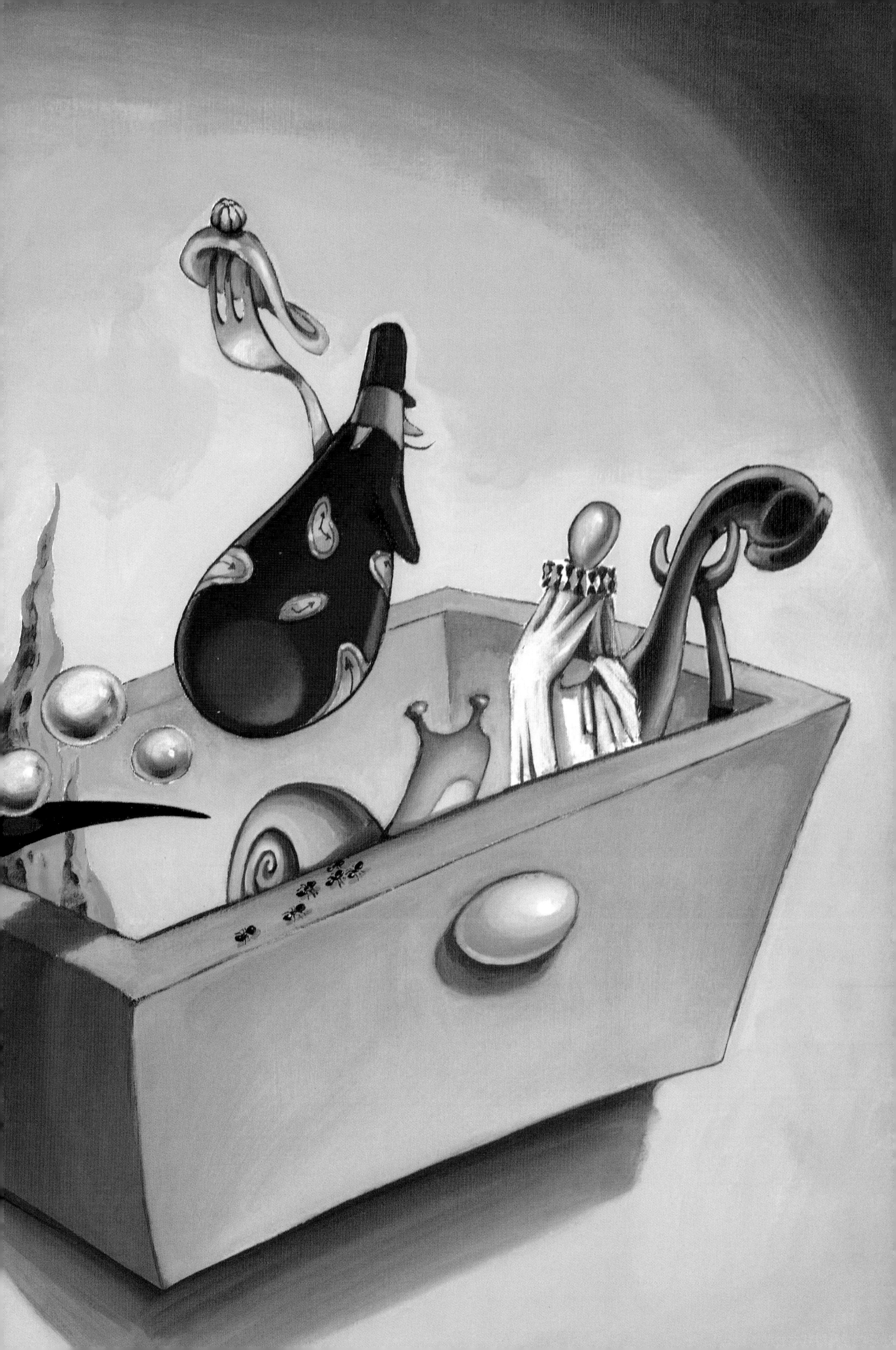

Like every child in the world, Salvi grew up. And then he wasn't known as Salvi any more, but Salvador Dalí. Although he was grown up, he never wanted to forget those dreamy afternoons of his childhood, and he decided to open the special drawer and paint the story of each of the people who lived inside.

So today, when we look at the paintings of Salvador Dalí, we can all share a part of those wonderful dreams.

Salvador Dalí

Once upon a time a boy called Salvador Dalí was born in Figueres near Girona in Spain, in the Spring of 1904.

Dalí was creative at an early age – he did his first painting at home on the wall of the laundry room. It is said that his first job as an artist was to create a little model carriage for the Three Kings in a nativity scene, to celebrate their arrival on 6th January, which is the most magical night of the year in Spain.

Dalí dreamed of being a chef, or maybe a great general like Napoleon, but when the time came he chose to study painting. and travelled to Paris and later to New York.

In Paris, Dalí met a group of artists who called themselves the Surrealists. They were inspired by dreams and the world of the unconscious.

The story goes that in Paris, Dalí met Gala, his fairytale princess. She became his muse, his model and his wife. They lived together in a fisherman's shack next to the sea at Port Lligat in Spain. They decorated their house with all sorts of strange objects, and people said that if you made it past the polar bear who guarded the front door, the inside was more like a maze in a dream than a real house!

As well as being a painter, Dalí was a writer, a stage designer, a jeweller, a book illustrator and a film director, but however he worked he always tried to capture a new world that had never been seen before.

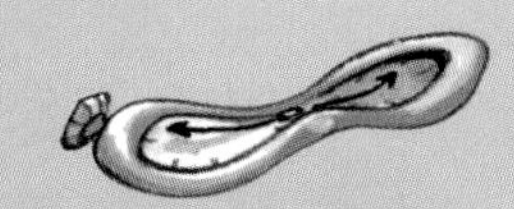

MORE TITLES FROM FRANCES LINCOLN CHILDREN'S BOOKS

Almost Famous Daisy

Richard Kidd

"Grand Painting Competition – My Favourite Things" announces the poster and so Daisy decides to enter. Her journey of discovery takes her around the world introducing her to favourite themes by Van Gogh, Monet, Chagall, Gauguin and Jackson Pollock, using reproductions from some of their most famous paintings.

Dogs' Night

Meredith Hooper

Illustrated by Allan Curless and Mark Burgess

It is Dogs' Night in the art gallery, the dogs' secret special night when they climb down from their paintings and chase one another around the gallery. They do this every year and no-one has ever found out. But on this particular night the dogs get over-excited and some of them end up in the wrong paintings!

Celebrity Cat

Meredith Hooper

Illustrated by Bee Willey

It's Cats' Visiting Night at the art gallery and all the city's cats have gathered to look at cat paintings. But there's hardly a painted cat to be seen! Felissima Cat ponders the problem and, paintbrush in paw, decides to put cats where they rightly belong…